THE
MAGICAL
ENVELOPE

Written and illustrated by
Nathenial Adams and Delilah Adams
Managed by Miriam Gonzalez-Adams

themagicalenvelope.com
ISBN # 9781737943327
Copyright 2021

Dedication

From Mom and Dad to Nathenial and Delilah
and to all the children in the world, always
know that no dream is too big to dream.

Delilah and Nathenial are twins. They have the same birthday, and they do a lot of things together. They like running around outside, and playing with toys inside.

They are happy kids, and
want other people to
be happy, too. Nathenia
and Delilah knew that
one way to make other
people happy was to
help others. They helped
their Mama carry in the
groceries, even if it was
just carrying a banana or
a box of cereal.

Now that they could read books, they could make stories come to life every time they read a book.

It gave them ideas for their own stories. When they played, they could pretend to be whatever they imagined. Pirates. Astronauts. Superheroes. Fairies. Firefighters. Princesses.

They could write down their names. Soon they were able to write other words, so they could write their own stories. They could write letters and words with a pencil. They could also type messages on a phone or a computer, and send them to their family or friends.

One day, the twins were writing a card to their Daddy. They loved to talk to him on the phone or the computer, but it was also fun to send him a card. A card was something you could decorate, and when the person got it in the mail, they could hang it up and keep it forever.

Their Daddy was working far away in the military, where he was helping people. He liked getting cards from his son and daughter. Mama helped them put the card in the envelope.

Delilah and Nathenial were having so much fun writing, they wanted to make more cards. The twins came up with an idea. There were other people working far from home, so the kids wanted to write cards for lots of them, too.

They wrote big cards and small cards. Green cards and purple cards. Nathenial liked to draw animals on the cards, like lions or bears, and also rocket ships. Delilah liked to draw little symbols, like happy faces, stars, or hearts, and especially unicorns.

Mama and the twins brought all the cards to the mail carrier. He put the cards in his truck, and drove them back to his post office. The mail carrier said Daddy and the other men and women in the military would get their letters in a few days.

Mama was proud of her son and daughter for always being so nice to each other, to other kids, and to everyone. They had a healthy dinner, and then they climbed into bed.

That night, Delilah and Nathenial each lay sleeping in their beds, when Delilah rolled over on something. It felt like paper. It woke her up. It was the card she and her brother made for their father. "Nathenial, wake up!" Delilah said. "We made so many letters and mailed them all, but we left this one behind."

They both got sad, because this was the card for their Daddy. It was late at night, so they didn't want to wake up their Mama, and they didn't know what to do. They told each other it was okay to make mistakes, but still cried a little bit. Kids get sad sometimes, and that's okay.

Their tears fell down on the envelope, and Nathenial and Delilah fell back to sleep.

As they slept, something magical happened. The envelope came to life from the teardrops.

2 Kindness lane
Magical love, 12345

It was a happy little envelope, who looked down at the address written on its stomach, and said, "I have to go somewhere, and this is where I have to go!"

The envelope was able to squeeze out of the window. It jumped into the wind, and flew in the air. Below it was the town, which was quiet and pretty at night.

The wind blew it over the trees, and over the school. It flew down to where the post office was. It was late at night, but there were trucks still working, taking all the letters and cards to different places in the world.

"That is where I must go!" the envelope said. A mail carrier was loading a much bigger truck, to drive it to a much bigger post office.

The happy envelope landed in the big bag of letters.

Inside the truck, one of the other envelopes looked scared, so the happy envelope asked the scared envelope what was wrong. "It's dark in here," the other one said. Then the happy envelope smiled and said, "It's okay. You don't have to be afraid." The other envelope cheered up.

Most times, when people, animals, or envelopes are frightened, they just need somebody to tell them it's going to be okay.

The truck arrived at a big, noisy place, with beeping horns and loud machines. Envelopes were jumping on moving belts and going to all different places. The happy envelope looked down at its stomach, to read the address where it had to go. "These trucks are going to the airport, to fly envelopes across the ocean!" it said, as it got into another truck.

When the envelope got to the airport, it was a very busy place. People, suitcases, and letters were getting on all different airplanes. The envelope was about to get to the plane, when it noticed a woman looked very lost. Her hair was gray like Delilah and Nathenial's grandma.

← ✈ Gate 1-5
→ ✈ Gate 6-10
↖ ✈ Gate 11-15
↑ ✈ Gate 16-20
↓ 🧳 Baggage

Do you need help? The envelope asked her. Yes, she said. I lost my glasses, and now I can't read my plane ticket. Can you tell me which plane to get on? The envelope was good at reading, so it was able to look at it and say,"Follow Me!"

Once the woman was on her plane, the envelope got on its airplane, and off it went, into the sky.

The mail carrier in the next country were loading up their trucks. It was exciting for the envelope to be in a new place. The envelope liked traveling, because it could meet new people.

Most people in the world were nice, no matter where they lived.

The envelope was in the mail truck, on its way to deliver the card to Delilah and Nathenial's Daddy.

When the truck stopped somewhere, the envelope saw a dog wandering in the street.

The envelope asked him, "Are you okay, doggy?"

The dog said he was lost. He had an address on his dog tag, but couldn't read his collar, because it looked upside down under his nose. The envelope laughed and said, "Don't worry. I can read it." The envelope told the doggy where to go, and the dog smiled, and barked a happy goodbye.

The envelope knew that when you do acts of kindness, you make the world a happier place.

Delilah and Nathenial's Daddy got a box of mail, with cards for all his friends. He handed them out, telling them that his kids made them.

The people at the military base were reading the nice cards that Delilah and Nathenial had made. They laughed at the cute pictures the twins drew, and the smiled at the nice things that Delilah and Nathenial wrote.

Their Daddy was looking around for a card for himself. Where was it?

Just then, the last envelope arrived. When Daddy opened the envelope, there was a card inside from Delilah and Nathenial, telling him they missed him, and loved him very much.

Delilah says...

"Giving back to others makes me feel happy because it makes the people we are helping happy. It's good to give back to others; everyone can do it too. One of my favorite things to do is to donate the toys I don't need anymore. I also like to help my mom and dad make food packages. I like to help our Military Heroes because making our Heroes feel happy makes me happy. It's always good to give back! You can make your own Magical Envelope and send it to someone to show them that being kind is nice. When you buy our book, you are helping my brother and I help, too."

Nathenial says...

"Giving back to others is a good and nice thing to do. Giving back makes me happy and makes the people we are helping happy too. Some of my favorite things to do are making sandwiches to help feed the less fortunate and drawing pictures on cards for Our Military or Veterans. I love helping our Military Heroes because they give so much of themselves to protect our Country. Remember to always give back and help others. When you buy our book, you are helping us to give back too."

We will be donating 10% of all our book sales to the MSAWI Organization in honor of our brave fallen hero, Major Stuart Adam Wolfer, who will never be forgotten.

2 Kindness Lane
Magical Love, 12345

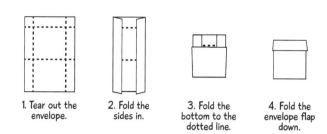

1. Tear out the
envelope.

2. Fold the
sides in.

3. Fold the
bottom to the
dotted line.

4. Fold the
envelope flap
down.

2 Kindness Lane
Magical love, 12345

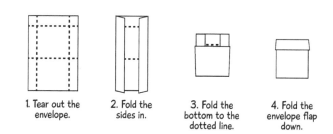

1. Tear out the envelope.

2. Fold the sides in.

3. Fold the bottom to the dotted line.

4. Fold the envelope flap down.

CPSIA information can be obtained
at www.ICGtesting.com
Printed in the USA
LVHW070932180822
726197LV00033B/373